Fraud Squad

Michele Martin Bossley

Orca currents

ORCA BOOK PUBLISHERS

Library and Archives Canada Cataloguing in Publication

Bossley, Michele Martin
Fraud squad / written by Michele Martin Bossley.
(Orca currents)

ISBN 978-1-55469-115-9 (bound).--ISBN 978-1-55469-114-2 (pbk.)

I. Title. II. Series: Orca currents
PS8553.O7394F73 2009   JC813'.54   C2009-902829-8

First published in the United States, 2009
Library of Congress Control Number: 2009928218

Summary: Robyn, Nick and Trevor learn about paleontology as they
try to solve a mystery at a local dinosaur dig.

MIX
Paper from
responsible sources
FSC® C016245
www.fsc.org

*Orca Book Publishers is dedicated to preserving the environment and has
printed this book on paper certified by the Forest Stewardship Council®.*

Orca Book Publishers gratefully acknowledges the support for its
publishing programs provided by the following agencies: the Government
of Canada through the Canada Book Fund and the Canada Council for the Arts,
and the Province of British Columbia through the BC Arts Council
and the Book Publishing Tax Credit.

Cover photography by Dreamstime

ORCA BOOK PUBLISHERS
PO Box 5626, Stn. B
Victoria, BC Canada
V8R 6S4

ORCA BOOK PUBLISHERS
PO Box 468
Custer, WA USA
98240-0468

www.orcabook.com
Printed and bound in Canada.

15 14 13 12 • 5 4 3 2

For Matthew, champion of children's literacy and fundraiser extraordinaire. Thank you so much for all your love and support.

Chapter One

A few feet from my face, huge jaws smiled menacingly, revealing curved sharp teeth perfect for tearing flesh. The creature looked ready to pounce if I moved so much as a baby finger.

"That is one big ugly dude," my cousin Nick said, shaking his spiky black hair out of his face. I jumped in spite of myself. Our friend Robyn repressed a shudder as she took in the blank eye sockets that seemed to look down from the bony skull.

The dinosaur skeleton had to be at least twenty feet tall. The neck swooped toward the floor, as if it were chasing smaller prey.

Our class was on a field trip, visiting the Royal Tyrrell Museum in Drumheller, Alberta. The Tyrrell Museum is famous for its fantastic dinosaur fossils. The badlands around Drumheller are some of the best dig sites for dinosaur fossils in the world.

Robyn, her freckled face scrunched into a frown, had made me promise before we left not to get us into any trouble at the museum. Like it's all my fault that weird things happen around the three of us. I have nothing to do with that. If anyone was to blame for getting us into sticky situations, it's Robyn. She's pretty nosy, even for a girl.

"He's one of the most complete spec-imens of the Tyrannosaurus rex ever found," Hailey Ross said. "My mom said it took years to find all the pieces."

"How do you know it's a he?" Robyn flicked her ponytail over her shoulder.

Hailey shrugged. "Females have a different substance in some of their bones. Paleontologists figured that out on a T. rex skeleton in Montana. Before that, we just guessed."

"Did your mom actually work on digging it up?" Nick asked.

"Yeah, she did. The digs are her favorite part. She likes teaching too though." Hailey glanced toward the front of the line, where her mom Jamie was leading the tour. "It's too bad that she might have to give that up." Hailey's expression hardened.

"Why?" I asked.

"We might be moving." Hailey's answer was so brief that I didn't want to ask anything more. Hailey was a nice kid. She never bragged, but we all knew that Dr. Ross had her name in the newspaper a lot when it came to important research in paleontology. Dr. Ross didn't look famous. She was dressed in khaki pants with multiple pockets, hiking shoes and a white blouse. She wore her brown hair cut blunt at her chin, just long enough to tuck behind her ears, and no makeup. Hailey looked a lot like her, except her hair was usually twisted into a long braid down her back.

Dr. Ross headed up important digs for the Tyrrell Museum, but she also spent part of her time at colleges and universities as a guest speaker.

I cleared my throat in the awkward pause that followed Hailey's comment and searched for something to say. "How come your dad didn't come today?" I asked at last. Hailey lived most of the time with her father in Calgary, which is why she went to our junior high. They commuted out to stay with her mom on the weekend. He had volunteered for some of our field trips last year.

"Because my mom said she would guide the tour with our class. She doesn't usually do them anymore," answered Hailey.

"Boys and girls," Dr. Ross called out. "I want to call your attention to this display. Do you notice the layers of rock surrounding this fossil? See how they are distinct colors. Each layer represents a different time in history. We call these *strata*. This is one way to date fossils."

The class began to drift over to the glass case that Dr. Ross pointed out, but I paused for another look at the giant bone structure. I leaned forward, holding onto the slick nylon band that held visitors back from the display. I wanted a closer look at those vicious teeth.

Without warning, the rope released with a sudden snap and retracted into the nearby steel pole.

"Whoa!" I teetered, about to do a major face-plant on the floor of the display.

"Trevor, don't!" Robyn cried as I grabbed hold of the only solid thing within reach—the dinosaur's lower jaw.

But it was too late. The dinosaur swayed. I held on instinctively, trying to steady myself with the huge bones. That was a big mistake. My weight made the dinosaur's jaw swing to the side, sending a ripple through the entire skeleton. The tail flapped once, as though the dinosaur was alive. I heard an awful groan as the bones loosened. Then the whole thing cratered.

Thud...thud...CRASH! The skeleton collapsed in a roar of noise. Bones rattled down. A few bounced crazily in all directions. Some kids had to duck.

I rolled out of the way as the huge skull dropped. Within seconds the impressive display was nothing more than a heap of old bones. Dust puffed from the crevices.

Coughing, I stared in horror at what I'd done. The rest of the class came running. Dr. Ross was right behind them.

"Holy bananas, Batman," Nick said, wide-eyed.

"Is everyone okay?" Dr. Ross shouted.

"What happened?" Nick asked, lifting the collar of his shirt over his nose and mouth as the dust thickened.

"I—" Dry-mouthed, I stopped. How could I ever explain?

"The rope broke," Robyn said. "I saw it. Trevor lost his balance and started to fall. He grabbed at something to get his balance and…"

"That happened to be the dinosaur skeleton," Nick finished. He groaned.

"Trevor, why do these things always happen to you?"

I shook my head miserably. I wished I knew.

"Oh well. It's not as bad as it seems," Dr. Ross said cheerfully.

"Not as bad as it seems?" Hailey gestured to the rubble in disbelief. "This is bad enough, isn't it?"

"Oh, it's a mess all right. But we'll get it cleaned up," said Dr. Ross.

"But what about all these broken fossils? They can't possibly be replaced," Robyn said. "Everybody knows how rare they are."

Dr. Ross started to laugh. "That's true. But these aren't fossils. They're plaster replicas!"

"What?" I gasped.

"We had them made for the children's display. The real fossils are in the central area of the museum. We put up a display that kids could get close to—

to see and touch. But kids were trying to climb on this guy, so we roped him off."

I found I could suddenly breathe again, in spite of the dust. "Really? This dinosaur was a fake?"

"Yup." Dr. Ross grinned. "As fake as the smile on a kid's face for school pictures!"

Chapter Two

"Hailey!" I said over the chatter in the classroom. I slid into my seat in science class. "When do you want to work on that booklet?" Our science teacher Mr. Kowalski had assigned us a bunch of work sheets about our visit to the museum, and Hailey was my partner.

Hailey waved her hand lazily. "It's not due until next week," she said.

"Yeah, but it's worth half our mark—" I began, but Mr. Kowalski's arrival stopped me.

"Hey kids! Settle down." Mr. Kowalski raised his voice. "I've got someone I want you to meet."

The room gradually became quiet. Standing near the front of the room was a blue-eyed guy who looked like he should be surfing. He wore a loose white polo shirt and baggy jeans. His dark blond hair hung in shaggy waves just above his shoulders. Some of the girls wore dopey grins as they stared at him.

"This is Mr. Johannsen," Mr. Kowalski introduced him. "He's joined the team of paleontologists at the Tyrrell Museum for the next few months. He's come to Alberta from South Dakota, where he also participated in dinosaur digs. Our school is very lucky to have him here. He will be working with us over the next month. I expect you to make him feel welcome."

An uncertain silence fell over the class. Mr. Johannsen smiled, showing a row of straight white teeth. "If it's okay with your teacher, I'd rather you guys call me Joe. Or Mr. Joe, if you feel the need. All right?" He looked at Mr. Kowalski.

"Sure, uh, Joe. No problem," Mr. Kowalski said.

"Cool." Mr. Joe nodded. "So, let's get down to it. I'm here to teach you about digging for old stuff. Like Mr. Kowalski already said, I've been on dig sites in the States, and I've even been on a few in Japan. I've dug up lots of old stuff, but my favorite is looking for dinosaur bones." His eyes brightened.

"I'm here as part of a scientist-in-residence program. I'm working toward a masters degree in paleontology. One of the things I've been looking at is a new fossil-dating technique that might turn out to be even better than carbon dating."

Mr. Joe pulled a fragment of bone out of his pocket. "This is one of the challenges scientists face. Can any of you tell how old this fossil is just by looking at it?"

The class shook their heads.

"Of course not. We have to find some way of measuring the molecular composition and comparing it to other fossils. That's what I'm working on. You guys catch that?"

We shook our heads again.

"That's okay. I'll explain it better when we have more time. For now, I can tell you how old this ancient fossil is." He held it up so everyone could see clearly. "Three weeks."

"What?" Nick said.

"It's chicken bone that has been *ossifying*—that's chilling out—for about three weeks. I do have some real fossils to show you, but we'll do that in the next session. We've got lots to talk about over the next few weeks, and all of it is awesome. I think you'll really be pumped."

"Is this guy for real?" Nick muttered to me out of the corner of his mouth.

I shrugged.

Mr. Kowalski nodded. "Right. Does anyone have questions for Mr. Joe before we go on to the regular lesson?"

Nick raised his hand. "What's your favorite part about the digs?"

An excited expression crossed Mr. Joe's face. "The discovery. Man, that rocks! There's nothing like it. It's like a treasure hunt for history. When you come across a dinosaur bone or a chunk of pottery from a different age, you're holding the years in your hand. It's an amazing feeling."

"Is it hard to find bones and things?" Robyn asked.

"Sometimes. Actually, lots of times. But there's kind of a knack to it. Some people just seem to have a feel for it... where stuff is in the soil. Intuition, I guess."

Hailey snorted. "I think it has more to do with luck. You just have to be in the right place."

Mr. Joe frowned. "Maybe. But there is some skill involved, you know. There's a brand-new site in Dinosaur Provincial Park that could be one of the richest sources of dinosaur fossils ever found in Alberta. We think we're in the right place, but we haven't found any fossils yet. And we may not get a chance to."

"Why not?" Robyn demanded.

"Because we haven't got enough money," Mr. Joe said bluntly. "The funding that's given to each museum or university to pursue their research isn't always enough to go toward new discoveries, especially a major one like this."

"But if this new site is so important, why can't the museum get more funding?" Robyn wanted to know.

"Well, we've applied for it, but there's only so much money," Mr. Joe said. "And the fact is, we don't really know that the site has tons of dinosaur fossils. We think it does, but we're only guessing." Mr. Joe shrugged, then gave us a wry grin. "If someone dug up a really rare fossil, we might be able to prove that the site should be a go."

"Isn't there another way to raise funds?" Hailey asked.

"There are private donations." Joe stretched out his hands in a helpless gesture. "But we can't count on that. If we don't get the money within the next three weeks, the dig will have to be shut down."

"I know." Hailey nodded. "My mom might have to work somewhere else if the funding doesn't come through." Her mouth pressed into a tight line.

Mr. Joe looked interested. "Who's your mom?"

"Jamie Ross," Hailey answered.

"Really? Jamie's your mom? Cool!" Mr. Joe said. "She's a great lady."

Robyn's forehead furrowed in thought. "What about fundraisers? Maybe we could help."

I repressed a groan. Fundraisers were Robyn's favorite events. Especially if she organized them.

"Hey, anything that helps the museum is great by me," Mr. Joe said. "But we're talking thousands of dollars."

"Well, if we could raise part of it, and people heard about the dig, that might help get more donations," Robyn reasoned.

"Sure. Raising awareness is always a good idea," agreed Mr. Joe. "Do you have any ideas?"

"Of course!" Robyn rubbed her hands together. "I was thinking about a school carnival. You know, where students set up booths for different activities — pie throwing, ring toss, games. Kids could buy tickets to do the activities they want. It could be really fun."

"I thought you wanted to do a carnival to raise money for an end-of-the-year picnic," Nick said.

Robyn waved that suggestion away. "Helping the museum is more important. We can have a picnic anytime."

Some of the kids looked unconvinced, but Hailey brimmed with enthusiasm. "We could invite the media," she said. "Maybe we could even get in the newspapers. Then people would really know about the new dig site!" Hailey beamed at Robyn. "It's a great idea."

Robyn had that determined look on her face that I knew so well. Nick and I exchanged glances of despair as she smiled. "Let's do it!" Robyn said.

Chapter Three

The gym buzzed with activity. Tables hung with streamers, and colored posters and decorations lined the gym in rows. Nick had rigged a pie-throwing station in one corner. Robyn, dressed in flowing gypsy skirts, hurried between booths, giving everything a last-minute check. "Trevor!" she called as she caught sight of me. "Isn't this terrific? Everyone's done something great."

I had to admit, it looked like fun. Most of Robyn's fundraising schemes involved Nick and I doing a whole lot of grunt work. But this time students signed up to run a booth, with the agreement that all proceeds would go toward the museum's planned dig site. The students decided what they wanted to do at their booth and set it up themselves. Mr. Kowalski had arranged to hold the carnival in the gym.

Some grade-nine girls had made beaded jewelry to sell. Another sold origami birds. Mr. Joe had set up a station with a bunch of rubber discs and a portable CD player.

"What's this?" I asked him.

"Musical whoopee cushions," Mr. Joe said.

"What do you do?"

"I play the music and everybody dances. When the music stops, everybody sits on a whoopee cushion. If you don't get one, or yours doesn't emit… uh…a gaseous noise, you're out. I eliminate a cushion each round until we're down to one, with two players left. It costs a dollar to play, and the winner keeps his cushion."

I snorted.

"Boys usually like this one," Mr. Joe said. "I'll have tons of customers."

"Do you think we'll raise enough money today to save the dig?" I asked.

Mr. Joe looked uncomfortable. "Uh…probably not quite enough. We need thousands, even with the government grant we're hoping to get. But it'll be a start. And if word gets out, maybe great things will happen."

"Maybe. Especially if Robyn and Hailey have anything to do with it." I grinned. "I'll be back later."

I walked around the gym, stopping where a small tent had been set up. The tent was draped with sheets covered with colorful swirls and designs cut from construction paper. I lifted the flap. "Robyn?"

Lit up by a flashlight covered in red cloth, Robyn's face had an eerie glow. Her hair was wrapped in a silk scarf, and her huge earrings sparkled in the dim light. "Robyn isn't here," she said in a gravelly voice. "Would you care to speak to Madame Robison instead?"

I tried not to laugh. "Madame Robison? That doesn't sound very mysterious, Robyn."

"Don't bug me," Robyn said in a normal tone. Then she resumed. "I am a teller of great fortunes. For a small fee"—she lowered her voice to a whisper—"I can reveal your future!"

"Yeah, sure," I said.

"Do you doubt me? Then give me your hand." Robyn reached for my palm. In spite of myself, I felt a shiver run down my spine.

"Yes," she rasped, "I see it now. You are very unlucky in jumping. You must guard against accidents in this respect. Beware!"

"If you're talking about the situation at the museum, I didn't jump on the dinosaur, I fell," I said. "And some fortune that is. You're not supposed to predict stuff that's already happened."

"You'll see," Robyn said. She adopted a grave expression. "The powers of the universe hold many secrets."

"I'll send in your next client," I replied, ignoring that last bit of wisdom. I pushed up the tent flap.

"Put up the In Session sign," Robyn called from inside the tent.

I propped up the cardboard sign as the next kid ducked eagerly inside.

A short line had formed outside the tent. The rest of the school had been allowed into the gym, and the carnival was now in full swing. I wandered among the booths, checking out the items for sale. One boy's homemade chocolate chip cookies were selling briskly. I bought one and munched on it as I walked.

Nick's pie-throwing station was busy, but most of the commotion came from Mr. Joe's musical whoopee cushions. I moved closer and watched. Mr. Joe started the music again. The kids danced, some of them awkwardly, others exaggerating the moves to make their friends laugh. As the song wore on, kids edged closer to the whoopee cushions. The music clicked off. Everybody dove for a cushion. A raucous noise filled the air.

"*Phhbbllat!*" the cushions said. Everyone laughed. One girl hadn't fought hard enough and found herself sitting on the floor. She was out.

"Next round!" Mr. Joe called.

Most of the kids opted not to play again, but there were others to take their place. I shook my head. The game was stupid, and probably better for younger kids, but it did look kind of funny. Besides, the money was for the dinosaur dig. I handed over some change and took a spot near a whoopee cushion in the corner.

Mr. Joe handed out clean straws and everybody blew up a cushion. Then he started the song.

At least the music's cool, I thought. I turned and found myself facing Hailey, who giggled at my dancing attempts.

When the music suddenly stopped, Hailey and I both jumped for the same cushion. Her knee knocked it sideways, and in the true spirit of competition, I leaped on it with both feet.

The cushion exploded in a flatulent noise of mammoth proportions and slipped out from under me. I skittered across the gym floor like I'd just stepped on a banana peel.

"Whoooaaa!" I cried, crashing into the booth next door, which happened to be selling dried macaroni bracelets. They rained down on top of me.

"Trevor, are you all right?" Mr. Joe asked.

"Yeah. What happened?" I sat up, picking a string of macaroni off my ear.

"Spit happened, that's what," he said as he examined the broken whoopee cushion. "When you jumped on this thing, you split it wide open. It's been blown up so many times it's slippery and wet on the inside. That must have been what came in contact with the floor. This rubber is normally so sticky, it would never have slipped."

I thought of Robyn's warning about being unlucky in jumping, and brushed it away. Splitting open a whoopee cushion could happen to anyone, right?

"Who's going to fix up this mess?" demanded the grade-nine girl from the ruined booth. "I have hardly anything left to sell!"

"Sorry," I muttered. "I'll help you clean up."

Mr. Kowalski came to investigate. Before I could move, a clamor of voices rose above the noise in the gym. A grade-seven girl ran up to Mr. Kowalski, panic etched on her face.

"What is going on?" he said in bewilderment.

"Robyn really is psychic!" the girl cried. "She just saved my life!"

Chapter Four

"Psychic or psycho?" Nick joked. "With Robyn, it would be hard to tell."

"Psychic?" Mr. Kowalski said. Around us, the carnival carried on in a thrum of noise. Only the kids nearest us had heard Alyssa's claim. "Alyssa, that's ridiculous. Robyn is definitely not psychic."

"I'm serious, Mr. K. She told my fortune, and within five minutes it came true. If she hadn't warned me, I'd be dead by now!" Alyssa gestured dramatically.

"What did Robyn tell you?" Hailey asked.

Alyssa glanced back. Robyn had left her tent and hurried toward us, her colorful skirts swirling around her legs. "She told me…" Alyssa answered, her voice shaking. She cleared her throat. "She told me to watch out for peanut-butter sandwiches!"

I stared at her. I wondered if I'd heard her correctly. "Huh?" I said.

"Peanut-butter sandwiches," Alyssa said loudly. "And then I was walking past the cookie booth. The boy had run out of chocolate-chip, and he asked if I wanted to try his new kind. I nearly bought one! I can't believe it!"

I shook my head, trying to understand Alyssa's weird logic. "What does that have to do with anything?" I said.

"It was peanut butter—the sandwich kind with two cookies and peanut-butter icing in the middle," Alyssa explained.

"So?" I said. By now, Robyn was listening.

"So I'm allergic to peanuts, you doof!" Alyssa yelled. Her patience was clearly at an end.

"Well, you never told us that," I said. But suddenly everything made sense. That's how Robyn's warning had saved Alyssa's life. A peanut allergy could be fatal, especially if it was severe.

I turned to Robyn. "Did you know she was allergic?"

Robyn shook her head. "No."

"So how'd you come up with a prediction like that?"

"I...just made it up. You know, I just tried to come up with ridiculous stuff. I had no idea she was allergic to peanuts."

"Well, you told me I was unlucky in jumping, and I just wiped out playing musical whoopee cushions. I nearly dislocated every bone in my body," I said.

"Really?" Alyssa pounced on that. "That's totally amazing! See, I told you Robyn was psychic!"

An excited buzz of conversation rose around us.

"No, I'm not," Robyn protested. "Really!"

A grade-seven boy tugged on Robyn's sleeve. "Can you tell me if I'll make the Division One hockey team?"

"No, I can't." Robyn pulled her arm away. "I can't answer questions like that."

"She can only give readings about things that jump into her mind," Alyssa said. "Isn't that right, Robyn?"

"Yes. No! I can't give readings at all. This is just supposed to be for fun. Like fortune cookies. Everyone knows that people can't really tell the future," Robyn said.

"Yeah? Then prove it," challenged Alyssa. "Do some more fortunes, and we'll see if they come true."

Nick nudged Robyn's elbow. "You could make a lot of money, Robyn. For the museum fundraiser."

"Well…" Robyn wavered.

"No one's really going to believe you can do it," I said, but I doubted my own words. Kids were staring with wide-eyed faith at Robyn, like she really was magic or something.

But Mr. Kowalski interrupted, clapping his hands for attention. "Kids, it's nearly time to clean up. I hope you've all had fun, but it's time to visit the last booths you want to see and then return to your classrooms for dismissal. Robyn, if you don't mind closing shop early, I have a couple of errands for you to do."

The crowd around us shuffled away, disappointed. Robyn looked relieved.

"What do you need me to do, Mr. K.?" she asked.

"Mr. Joe brought some forms from the museum that we need to fill out for this fundraiser. Could you go get them, please? Joe, where are they?"

Mr. Joe looked up from where he was picking up whoopee cushions. "Sitting on my desk in your classroom. They're the pink ones, Robyn."

"Okay," she said, walking toward the gym door. I followed her.

"You all right?" I asked her.

"Why wouldn't I be?" Robyn strode quickly down the hall, avoiding the stares of the other kids. Word was already spreading about Robyn's predictions.

"Well, it's kind of weird, don't you think?" I said. "Two predictions coming true like that?"

"Coincidence," Robyn answered firmly. "It was just luck."

I dropped the subject and entered the classroom. Mr. Joe's desk was an untidy table shoved into the back corner of the room. A small metal filing cabinet stood next to it. Everything was covered in layers of paper.

"He's only been here a few days. How could he make such a huge mess in a few days?" Robyn said.

I shrugged. "My mother asks me the same thing about my room."

"Do you see any pink forms?" asked Robyn. She gingerly moved aside a few sheaves of paper.

"There's some under there," I reached for some papers at the bottom of a stack near the corner of the table. As I tugged on them, the whole top of the stack cascaded over the filing cabinet and onto the floor.

"Trevor!" Robyn scolded.

"Sorry." I bent to pick them up. A few papers had lodged into the half-open filing-cabinet drawer. I opened the drawer to grab the papers. There were no files inside. Instead the papers rested on a black duffel bag. The zipper gaped open, and I could see clear plastic bags with what looked like old bones inside. One of the bags had a blue and white label stuck to it. It said *Ichthy. butt.*

I glanced at Robyn, puzzled. "Do you see that?" I asked.

She peered down. "Itchy butt? What does that mean?"

"I don't know. But they look like fossils to me. Why would Mr. Joe have fossils hidden in here?"

Robyn shrugged. "He's probably using them for teaching. I'll bet the Tyrrell Museum let him borrow them."

I leaned closer so I could see more clearly. The bags were filled with small chunks of what looked like brownish white oblong rocks. They were filmy with dust and smelled a bit like chalk. I noticed one of the labels had been ripped off, but the words were still legible.

I looked up at Robyn. "Oh yeah?" I told her. "Then why does that bag say *Property of the University of South Dakota*?"

Chapter Five

"I'm sure there's a reasonable explanation," Robyn answered with dignity.

"Like what?" I said suspiciously.

"Mr. Joe has every reason to have fossils with him," Robyn said flatly. "He's an instructor."

"Yeah, but you know as well as I do that fossils from South Dakota wouldn't be at the Tyrrell Museum," I countered.

"Well, maybe just the bag is from the University of South Dakota," Robyn insisted stubbornly. "Or maybe Mr. Joe has his own private collection."

"I don't know," I said slowly. "There's something I don't quite trust about him."

"What are you talking about? He's nice."

"You just like him because he's good-looking," I accused. The tip of Robyn's nose turned pink.

"Trevor!" Hailey called from the doorway. "The carnival's over. Mr. Kowalski needs help putting away all the tables from the booths."

"Why me?" I ask.

"Because the caretaker leaves early on Friday afternoons," Hailey answered. She walked over to us, her eyes widening as she saw the fossils in the cabinet. "What's that?" she said.

"Nothing." I shoved the drawer shut with my foot. "We were just looking for the museum forms. Can you get them for Mr. Joe?" I asked Robyn.

She frowned. "Of course. I think I can do a simple thing like that without you."

"Sure. *If* you can find them in this mess." I glanced at Mr. Joe's untidy desk.

"It wasn't so messy before you dumped half the papers on the floor," Robyn grumbled. She began sifting through a mound of paper, and Hailey and I took off to help Mr. Kowalski in the gym.

"Robyn. Robyn!" a girl shouted over the clamor in the hallway on Monday morning. I recognized her as a friend of Alyssa's. "Robyn, you have to do a prediction for me. I need to know—"

What she needed to know was cut off by another girl shoving her way toward us.

"Listen, Robyn, I really need to talk to you. Can you meet me after school?" Her eyelids were heavily rimmed with black eyeliner. She wore black clothing from head to toe. I knew she was in grade nine, but I'd never spoken to her before.

"Well, uh…I don't know," Robyn hedged.

"Listen, it's okay." The girl touched Robyn's sleeve gently. "What you can do is totally amazing. Only really special people have the gift. And it can't be forced. If you can't see anything for me, that's cool." She smiled.

Robyn looked embarrassed and pleased at the same time. "Well, maybe."

"I'll see you at your locker. 3:15. Don't forget." The black-clad girl moved off down the hallway. Robyn drew a deep breath. "This is really getting out of hand."

"You're becoming quite a celebrity," I observed.

"People should have more common sense," Robyn snapped. "Fortune-telling isn't real."

"They think it is," I said. "And that's what counts. People really believe you can do it."

Mr. Joe stopped us next. "Robyn, could I talk to you and Trevor for a minute, please?" His face looked so serious that Robyn and I glanced at each other in alarm.

"What's the matter, Mr. Joe?" Robyn asked.

Mr. Joe rubbed a hand through his hair. "On Friday when you picked up the fundraiser forms from my desk, did you notice anything else?"

"What do you mean?" I asked.

"I mean like whether the filing cabinet was open or not," Mr. Joe said.

"It was," Robyn admitted. "Trevor knocked a bunch of papers off your desk, and some of them fell inside the cabinet. We pulled them out and put them back right away though," she added quickly.

"That's good. But I'm more worried about what was in the cabinet. I can't believe I didn't lock it," Mr. Joe said, more to himself than to us.

"What happened?" I said.

"Did you see anything…else… inside the cabinet?" Mr. Joe said.

Robyn and I exchanged looks. "There were some plastic bags with a bunch of rocks inside," I answered.

Mr. Joe exhaled. "So they were still there on Friday afternoon." He shook his head. "Those rocks were fossils on loan to me. I brought them to show the students here at the school. But now they're missing," Mr. Joe said.

I noticed he didn't mention anything about the University of South Dakota label.

"If you guys know anything about the fossils at all, I need to find out. They're very valuable," Mr. Joe pressed us.

"Hey, Robyn, maybe you could predict where they are. You've done okay so far, telling fortunes," I joked.

Robyn scowled at me.

"I'm serious, Trevor," Mr. Joe said. "This is a big deal."

"We saw the fossils inside the bag before I went back to the gym to help clean up. There were quite a few inside a black duffel bag. But we never touched them. Right, Robyn?" I answered.

Robyn's face grew red. I looked at her quizzically. "No, that's right," she said quickly. "I did look at them again after I found the museum forms, and then I shut the cabinet."

"Did you lock it?" Mr. Joe said hopefully.

Robyn shook her head. "It wasn't locked before, so I just pushed it closed."

Mr. Joe sighed. "All right. I'll have to make an announcement. I need those fossils back. My career could depend on it!" He strode off down the hallway in the direction of the office.

Nick had joined us in time to hear Mr. Joe's last comment. "He's right," Nick said. "Because if he doesn't come up with those fossils, he might be going to jail."

"What?" Robyn gasped. "What are you talking about?"

Nick handed her a sheaf of computer printouts. "I was just in the library working on my science booklet, and I ran an Internet search. By the way, did you know that some scientists think the Ichthyosaur was a giant marine reptile that evolved from a land reptile that no one knows anything about?

Robyn rolled her eyes. "Get to the point, Nick!"

"It was during the Triassic period. Isn't that kind of cool? I mean, they were on land, then whoops…they developed fins or something and jumped into the sea. I never knew dinosaurs were this cool." Nick grinned.

"Nick! Mr. Joe…jail…remember? What were you going to tell us?" Robyn looked as though she might throttle Nick at any moment.

"Oh, yeah. Well anyway, I was searching all this stuff, and I found a newspaper story from South Dakota that said someone ripped off a bunch of fossils a few months ago."

"I knew it!" I exclaimed.

"No way." Robyn shook her head. "There has to be some mistake."

"Think about it," Nick said. "The guy shows up here from that exact university, and suddenly he has a bunch of rocks from their collection? Sounds suspicious to me."

"Why would he leave them labeled then? Isn't that totally stupid? Of course someone would figure it out," Robyn argued.

"He did say the fossils were on loan to him," I pointed out.

"And what about customs officers when Mr. Joe came across the border?" Robyn said. "Wouldn't they have stopped him?"

"Who knows?" Nick shrugged. "Maybe he didn't store them in the bags, and the security guys just thought Mr. Joe has some weird habit of collecting gravel. But I'm telling you, it's way too much of a coincidence. Check out how much money the article says they'd be worth to a private collector!" He waved the computer printout under my nose.

"Ten thousand dollars?" I gasped. "Are you kidding? For old rocks?"

"Old fossils," Nick reminded me, reading over my shoulder, "that are obviously really rare."

Our next class was about to begin. We stepped through the doorway to find an excited knot of kids clustered around Hailey. She was gesturing wildly, but froze when she saw us. Immediately everyone else grew quiet, their eyes on Robyn.

"What's going on?" I said.

"Another one of Robyn's prediction's came true," Hailey said.

Robyn looked apprehensive. "Which one?"

"The one you gave me," Hailey answered. "Remember, you said yellow school buses were a problem for me?"

I started to laugh. "Yellow school buses are a problem? How stupid is that?"

Robyn gave me a thin smile, but Hailey's face remained serious. "I thought so too. But guess what?

This morning the buses pulled up to the school for the second field trip to Drumheller. And look what they did." Hailey pulled up a battered, squashed backpack. Tire-tread marks ran right down the middle.

"I dropped it by accident, and it rolled off the curb, just as the buses pulled up. Before I could grab it…well, you can see what happened. It wrecked the whole backpack and everything in it, including my lunch." Hailey's eyes widened. "But at least it was only my backpack, and not me!"

Chapter Six

The gravel road to the park near Drumheller gave way to a rutted, bumpy track.

"I wonder if Mr. Joe tracked down the fossils yet," Nick said from across the aisle. Mr. Joe hadn't come on the bus with us. He planned to stay at the dig after we were finished, so he'd taken his own car. "Hey, Robyn," yelled a girl who was sitting with Hailey, "will you tell my fortune next?"

"Sure," Robyn turned, nearly hitting her chin on the back of the seat as the school bus bucked again. "For five bucks."

"That's pretty expensive," the girl said.

"It's worth it. Ask Hailey," Robyn replied. "Besides, I'm giving the money to the museum." She turned back to me. "We only made seven hundred and thirty-two dollars at the carnival," she said in an undertone.

"That's not nearly enough," I said.

"I know." Robyn frowned. "I really hoped we could raise more money. I sure hope that funding comes through."

"Me too. For Hailey and her mom, especially." I glanced back.

Hailey saw me watching her and suddenly slapped her forehead with her palm.

"Trevor, did you do your part of the study questions for our science booklet last night?" she called over the noise in the bus.

"Yeah. We were supposed to hand them in this morning, but Mr. Kowalski forgot to collect them," I answered.

"Can you help me figure out page four? It's the only one I didn't get finished. Mr. Kowalski's going to ask for them before dismissal, and it's worth fifty percent our grade."

"I know," I told her as I switched seats. "I told you that last week."

Hailey ignored that and pulled the work sheet from her binder, laying it on the smooth cover.

"You did the calculation wrong," I said, reading her answers. "Check the numbers in question three on the examples of fossil age. See, you substituted the wrong thing." Hailey erased her work and redid it, her pen shooting off in all directions with each jolt of the bus.

"There," she said, pleased. "It's messy, but at least now it's right. I worked on this one for, like, an hour last night. I brought it this morning, because I wanted to ask you before class. But then the school bus thing kind of threw me off."

"Yeah, I bet," I said. Something about Hailey's homework bugged me. I couldn't quite put a finger on it. It was more than the fact that she'd left it to the last minute, which could mean that we'd both get a bad mark.

The bus bounced and creaked over the ruts, grinding to a halt in a rough clearing.

"Okay, kids," Mr. Kowalski said. "We've been given a very special privilege today, because of Hailey's mom and her work with the Tyrrell Museum. Most schools would not be invited to get

I stepped down the plywood stairs leading to the dig site. Hailey's mom was waiting for us. She dusted her hands off on her jeans.

"Hi, kids," Dr. Ross greeted us, smiling. She had sunglasses perched on the top of her head. "Everybody ready to do some digging?"

We filed down into the dusty clearing. Dr. Ross handed each of us a tool. Some people got brushes. Others were given small shovels and an assortment of other tools. I took my brush and waited for instructions.

"We dig very carefully at a paleontology site. If we're not careful, we could ruin fossils, so it's important to follow directions. Nobody is to do anything without a supervisor," Dr. Ross said. "I'd like us to split into three groups. I'll work with one, and Joe and Mr. Kowalski will work with the other two."

"Mr. Joe's not here yet," Hailey said.

"Well, we'll get started and break up into a third group when he gets here," Dr. Ross decided. "Trevor, would you step over here, please? We'll demonstrate how to go about the dig." She used her trowel to carefully scrape the hardened soil, loosening it gently.

"See how I'm not forcing the shovel into the earth?" she said. "That could chip or break a fragile fossil. Move the dirt gently, then use the brushes to sweep it away." She motioned for me to kneel beside her. I took the soft brush and swept the dirt to the side.

"See? There's the beginning of a bone." Dr. Ross pointed. The rest of the class crowded around to see. "I was working at this site earlier, and I knew we had something here."

I looked, but all I could see was more dirt and a lump in the middle.

"If we work at this," she said, "we may be able to unearth the whole thing before you leave." Dr. Ross took her trowel and loosened more dirt around the lump of bone. As she bent to flick some of the larger clods away with her fingers, I heard the thuds of footsteps.

Mr. Joe was rushing down the rickety stairs. He arrived with a breathless thump, his lips drawn in a grim line.

Mr. Kowalski marshaled our attention. "Okay, kids. I'm going to count you off into groups. If you're a one, you'll be with me, twos will go with Mr. Joe and threes will be supervised by Dr. Ross."

Dr. Ross stood up and stepped quickly over to Mr. Joe. I edged sideways behind her, straining to catch what they were saying.

"What's the matter?" I heard Dr. Ross mutter.

"I stopped at the office on the way in," Mr. Joe said under his breath. "The funding we were expecting has been slashed to practically nothing!"

Chapter Seven

Five glum days later, Robyn and I waited for the morning bus to school. She kept kicking morosely at the curb with her heel, lost in thought.

"Robyn, you have to snap out of it. We gave it a good try with the carnival, but the dig needs more money than we could ever raise," I said, trying to be comforting.

"I know that," Robyn snapped. "But I wish we could do more. Ever since you told me what Mr. Joe said about losing the funding, I've been in a bad mood."

"No, really?" I said with mock innocence. I ducked as Robyn clubbed me with her backpack.

Nick rounded the corner, his shoelaces flapping, spiky hair uncombed and a newspaper shoved in his open backpack. "You guys—wait till you hear this!" he gasped.

"What happened—you sleep through your alarm again?" I asked.

"No. Yes! But that's not the point. Look!" He reached into the backpack and pulled out the newspaper. Splashed across the front page was a picture of the dinosaur dig, with Mr. Joe grinning in the middle. The headline shouted, *Major Fossil*

Find in Drumheller. I scanned the beginning of the article.

Paleontologists were ecstatic yesterday to identify a bone unearthed at a new dig site in Drumheller as belonging to a dinosaur never before discovered in Alberta. The fragment of bone, identified as part of an Ichthylobuttosaur skeleton, is the first ever found in this province.

"The significance of this find is huge," said Dr. Jamie Ross, PhD, the director of the dig. "The Ichthylobuttosaur is a relatively unknown dinosaur, found mainly in the Black Hills area of South Dakota."

The Ichthylobuttosaur has previously been thought of as strictly a marine reptile, but this new discovery could turn that theory on its ear.

Ryan Johannsen, who joins the team from the University of South Dakota, unearthed the fossils.

"I've never been so excited about a find," Johannsen said. *"World interest in this is going to be huge."*

"This discovery could mean that the Ichthylobuttosaur migrated from Alberta to South Dakota through an as yet unknown waterway. It also may represent evidence that Mesozoic marine reptiles evolved from land reptiles. If they couldn't travel by water, then how else did they get here?" asked Dr. Ross. *"This is an absolutely amazing find. We're all thrilled."*

The dig site, which, according to Johannsen, contains a potential gold mine of fossils, is scheduled to close next week due to lack of funding. The new discovery has reopened the issue of government funding toward maintaining the dig site. Politicians were not yet able to comment on whether funds could be made available.

"That's great!" Robyn bubbled, her first smile in days stretching across her face.

"Who is this Ryan Johannsen guy anyways?" I asked.

"That's Mr. Joe, doofus," said Robyn. "It's so cool that he found the fossil. He was just saying how a major find could save the dig!"

Nick narrowed his eyes. "I don't think this is a major find at all. Robyn, don't you find it just a little too much of a coincidence that a big discovery like that happened just when we needed it? Especially when the Ichthylobuttosaur has never been discovered outside of South Dakota? And Mr. Joe has just come from South Dakota? Come on!"

Robyn stared at him.

I tracked Nick's thoughts. "And we found fossils in his filing cabinet that were marked 'Itchy butt, University of South Dakota.' Ichthylobuttosaur. I get it. You're saying he planted those fossils at the dig to get publicity for more funding."

"That's stupid!" Robyn argued. "It would be obvious after a few months, when no more Ichthylobuttosaur bones were found, that the whole thing was a sham."

"By then, the funding would have come through. And maybe Mr. Joe's counting on another major discovery— a real one—to justify the whole thing. He really believes that the dig is important," Nick said. "So maybe he's just trying to buy time."

"Illegally," I added.

"How is it illegal, exactly?" Robyn wanted to know.

"Well, it must be fraud, misrepresenting those fossils like that. It's dishonest, for sure," I answered.

"And if no one figured it out, a major discovery like that could make a pale-ontologist's whole career."

"But I *like* Mr. Joe. I can't believe he would do something like that," Robyn protested.

I didn't respond. The three of us just stared at the newspaper article as if it might offer more answers. But no other solutions made sense. Mr. Joe was the only person who could be responsible if the discovery was phony.

"We need to find those fossils," I said.

Robyn hesitated. "But Trevor, if they're not all buried at the dig site, they could be anywhere. It would be like looking for a needle in a haystack now."

I fixed her with an unmoving stare. "Since when did that ever stop you?"

Before she could answer, Cray Simmons walked up. "Hey, Robyn," he called out. "What's the deal? You setting up another big prediction?" Teasing Robyn was his favorite hobby.

She whirled around. "What are you talking about?" she demanded.

"Rumor has it that you're a fake." Cray raised one eyebrow.

"I heard that too," a short grade-seven girl piped up. "But I didn't believe it," she added.

A guy I knew from gym class broke in. "My friends say it's all a scam to make money."

"Well, of course it is!" Robyn rounded on them in fury. "I did it for the school carnival. I never claimed I could really tell fortunes. People just ended up believing it."

"Yeah, but now some kids really think you're psychic," Cray leered. "It's social suicide to admit you aren't."

"Well, that's just super," Robyn said sarcastically. "I didn't want them to believe I had supernatural powers, and now that they do, it's my fault if I admit I can't tell fortunes?"

"Pretty much, yep." Cray grinned. "I heard that you knew some of those fortunes ahead of time, like the fact that Alyssa Mercer is allergic to peanut butter. So you set up fortunes that *had* to come true."

"That's a total lie!" Robyn flushed hotly.

"Yeah!" I said. "Robyn told me to beware of jumping. How is that supposed to be a setup?"

"That's not a setup, that's a no-brainer. Everyone knows you're a klutz," Cray sniggered.

The bus pulled up. Robyn, Nick and I climbed aboard. We took a seat far away from Cray, but there was no mistaking the sudden silence and covert whisperings as Robyn made her way down the aisle.

She flopped into a seat near the back. "I don't believe this!" she wailed. "Now what am I going to do?"

I shrugged and tried to look sympathetic. "Buy a crystal ball?"

Chapter Eight

I walked up to Robyn's locker in the crowded hallway the next morning at school. "Hey," I said.

She jumped a mile. "Holy Jeez, Trevor!" Robyn clenched her hands, scrunching a piece of paper into a ball. "You scared me!" Her breath came in gasps.

I stared at her in surprise. "What's the matter with you? You'd think I was wearing a vampire costume or something."

Robyn gave a nervous laugh. "You just…surprised me, that's all." She reached for her books. "I have to hurry. I need to see Mr. Joe before class." She slammed the locker door, locked it and strode off.

"Weird," I said, shaking my head as I watched her go.

"What is?" Nick joined me.

"Robyn," I answered.

"Well, yeah. That's obvious. You haven't figured that out yet?"

"No, I mean she's acting weird. She ran off like she was avoiding me or something."

"Well, your breath *is* kind of bad," Nick joked. "When's the last time you flossed?"

I frowned. "She said she needed to talk to Mr. Joe before class, but she just went the opposite direction, away from the classroom."

I watched Robyn at the end of the hallway snaking through knots of kids, glancing from side to side. She ducked through the doors leading to the stairwell into the basement.

"Let's follow her," Nick said suddenly. "She's definitely up to something. Maybe she has a lead on the missing fossils."

"If she has a plan to catch somebody, we could mess it up if we go after her," I answered.

"Yeah, but Trev, you know Robyn. She could be getting herself into more than she bargained for. I say we stick together."

"Okay," I agreed. "Let's go."

We hurried down the hall to the stairwell door we'd seen Robyn disappear through. Some of the kids were heading to class, but we still had a few minutes before the bell, so a lot of the kids were just standing around talking.

We let the door shut behind us softly and crept down the stairs. These stairs weren't used often. The only time students went to the basement was to use the locker rooms for gym, and they were at the opposite end of the building.

At the bottom of the stairwell, a closed door led to another corridor, but movement under the stairs caught my attention. I nudged Nick and peered into the dim light. A familiar form emerged, clutching something with both hands.

"Robyn?" I said uncertainly.

"Trevor?" Robyn's voice shook. I could see the fear in her eyes. She was holding plastic bags filled with bulky objects.

I could see clearly through the transparent bags. Robyn had the missing fossils.

Chapter Nine

Thoughts crashed through my brain, colliding with such speed that I couldn't grasp them. Robyn had the missing fossils. Why was she down here in the basement alone under the stairwell? How did she know where to find the fossils?

"Robyn, what are you doing?" I demanded.

Robyn shrank back. "I came down to get these." She held up the bags. "I found a note in my locker telling me to come down here and get them."

"Why?" I asked.

"Because the note said I had to return the fossils to Mr. Joe or I'd be revealed as a total fortune-telling fraud in front of the whole school."

I glanced at Nick. I read the doubt in his face. I knew what he was thinking, because I was thinking it too. Could Robyn have stolen the fossils? But why would she?

"How could they possibly do that?" I said.

Robyn was near tears. "The note said they would tell everyone I had stolen the fossils so I could make a prediction about them and then 'find' them, so everyone would believe I was really psychic. They said they would tell everyone that I'm a liar."

"So where is this note?" Nick wanted to know.

"I threw it out," Robyn answered miserably. "I didn't want anyone to see it."

"Uh-huh." The skepticism in Nick's voice was obvious.

"Listen, Nick, just what are you implying?" Robyn flared. "That I took the fossils myself? You think maybe I'm going to sell them on eBay or something? Get real!"

Nick folded his arms across his chest. "Sounds like a confession to me."

"Trevor?" Robyn focused her pleading eyes on me. "You believe me, don't you?"

But I didn't know what to believe. I didn't think Robyn would take the fossils. But seeing them in her hands made it hard to take her word for it. Besides, the note story seemed a little far-fetched. Who would target Robyn?

Robyn read the hesitation in my silence. "You guys!" she cried. "You're impossible. I'm taking these to Mr. Joe right now. And then I'm going to find out who wrote that note."

"Good luck," Nick muttered. "Now that you threw it away, you have no evidence."

Robyn ignored him and started up the stairs. I followed her slowly, with Nick at my heels.

"You really think she took them?" I whispered.

Nick shrugged. "I dunno. But she's acting pretty weird."

"Wouldn't you, if someone threatened to humiliate you in front of the whole school?" I said.

"Maybe," Nick said. "If that's even true. Robyn could be making the whole thing up."

I pushed open the door at the top of the stairs and went straight to Mr. Joe's desk at the back of our classroom. Robyn was already there. Mr. Joe stared at her, open-mouthed, as she placed the bag of fossils in front of him.

"Robyn! You found them! That's great!" he said. Mr. Joe lifted up each plastic zippered bag, examining the fossils. "I've been stressed about losing these guys. I kept hoping they'd turn up. Where were they?"

Robyn glared at us as we crossed the room and stood beside her. "They were hidden underneath the stairwell in the basement," she said. "Someone left a note in my locker that told me where they were."

"Really?" Mr. Joe's gaze wavered. "That's odd. What did the note say?"

"That if I didn't return the fossils, they'd tell the whole school that all my predictions were a lie."

"Hmmm," Mr. Joe said. I couldn't read his expression. "Well, I'd just forget it. I doubt the note writer was serious. It's probably all a joke. Maybe someone took the fossils as a prank and was too scared to bring them back."

"I'm not sure it was a prank," I said. "Maybe we should file a report with the police."

Mr. Joe's face registered alarm. "Oh, I don't think that's a good idea. We've got the fossils back. Why bug the police when it could have been a mistake? Maybe one of the janitors thought he was getting rid of some old junk or something."

"By hiding them under the stairs?" Nick sounded skeptical.

"And why would a janitor leave a note for Robyn?" I asked.

"You know what I mean. It's probably nothing to get worked up about," Mr. Joe said.

Robyn's face had whitened at the mention of the police. "Well, I'm glad

I found the fossils for you," she said. She turned and pushed past us.

"Is she okay?" asked Mr. Joe.

"I think so," I answered. "Besides this mystery note, she's been a little testy about how the fundraiser bombed."

"Aren't we all," Mr. Joe said. "Not that I expected you kids to make up the shortfall. It was great of the students to want to help out. But we could be on the brink of some fantastic discoveries out there. I'm hoping that the news of the Ichthylobuttosaur find sways the politicians into allocating more funds before the dig shuts down."

"That would be terrific," I said. "See you later, Mr. Joe. We're late for gym." I pulled Nick back through the doorway.

"What's the big idea?" Outside, Nick pulled away from my grasp.

"I want to see if Robyn talks to anyone before class—or if anyone's watching her."

"You don't really buy that note garbage, do you?" Nick scoffed.

"I don't know." I glanced down the now empty hall. We really werc late for gym, but I figured a few more minutes wouldn't matter.

I'd spotted something important. I nudged Nick. We headed toward a trash can partway down the hall. It had an unusual appearance—two legs and a backside were sticking out of the top. Someone was rummaging around inside.

We watched as Robyn emerged from the trash can. Her hair was a mess, something orange and globular ran down her shirt, but she had a triumphant expression on her face. "Hah!" she said when she saw us. "Here's your evidence, *Nick*!" Her voice dripped sarcasm as she flung a wad of soggy paper at Nick's head.

Nick ducked, and the damp projectile hit me instead. "Yuck!" I yelped, peeling it off my cheek. I gingerly opened it to find a juice-soaked typewritten note. The ink had slid into streaks, making the entire thing unreadable. I raised my eyebrows and looked at Nick, who was also studying the illegible note.

Robyn folded her arms across her chest, ignoring the disgusting blob on her shirt. "I told you I wasn't lying," she said. "Someone is out to get me!"

"But, Robyn"—I shook off a few bits of orange peel and waved the page at her—"this proves nothing. We can't even read it!"

Chapter Ten

Robyn still wasn't speaking to us. Nick claimed it was a welcome relief and the most relaxing two days he'd ever had, but I could tell he felt bad. I did too. Unfortunately, there was only one way to fix things.

"Get real, Trev," Nick said when I told him what we had to do. "How are we going to figure out who wrote that note?

Haven't we got enough to do, trying to prove that Mr. Joe planted the fossils at the dig, without adding Robyn's mystery note to the mix?"

"Maybe we can do both," I said slowly. "I have a feeling the two are connected."

"What's connected?" Hailey asked as she slipped into the seat in front of me. Science class should have started ten minutes ago, but there was still no sign of Mr. Joe.

I hesitated. I wasn't sure we should tell anyone about our suspicions, but Hailey's mom worked at the dig too. Hailey probably had a good idea what went on up there. As briefly as possible, I explained about Robyn and the mystery note. I told her we suspected Mr. Joe had planted the fossil at the dig. Hailey scowled as I talked.

"I think there might be a connection there, somehow," I finished.

"No way," Nick scoffed. "Mr. Joe would never leave a note threatening to trash Robyn's reputation. The guy's an adult. That's something a kid would do."

"I know. I'm not saying he did it. But there's got to be a connection," I answered. "The South Dakota fossils were missing from Mr. Joe's filing cabinet, along with the rest. But I didn't see them in the bag Robyn found under the stairs. I looked when Mr. Joe held them up."

"So what are you saying?" Hailey asked.

"That whoever stole the fossils didn't take the ones from South Dakota, or they didn't leave them for Robyn to find." I said. Robyn sat nearby, pretending to ignore us, but I knew she heard every word we said.

"Of course they didn't," Nick scoffed. "Because Mr. Joe had already removed the South Dakota fossils before they were stolen."

"How? Why? They were all in the filing cabinet on Friday afternoon. Mr. Joe was cleaning up at the carnival. He left when we did. Then Monday morning before class, he asked us if we'd seen them. Someone swiped them Friday after school. Mr. Joe wouldn't have had time to take the Ichthylobuttosaur fossils," I said.

"Unless he came back later," Robyn broke into the conversation.

"I thought you weren't talking to us," Nick said.

"I'm not," Robyn answered grimly. "But I intend to prove my innocence."

"Mr. Joe couldn't come back later. The school is locked after four thirty," I said. "And he was very upset about the missing fossils."

"Sometimes the school is opened for clubs or sports teams," Nick argued.

"It had to be Mr. Joe. He's the only one who has access to both the dig and the fossils. And he's the only one with a good reason for doing it. His 'discovery' is getting major publicity. That will get more funding for the dig and it will probably vault his career into the stratosphere. Everyone's going to think he's a genius."

I was silent. Everything Nick said made sense. It was the same argument that I'd thought of as well.

"I think we need to go out there," Robyn announced.

"What?" Hailey said, startled. "Where?"

"The dig site. That's where all the action is," answered Robyn. "If we're going to find any proof, that's where it will be. The newspaper said only a few fossils were found. That means there are more. Maybe Mr. Joe didn't get a chance to plant all of them. If we could catch him in the act, we'd have proof for sure."

"Sounds great," Nick said sarcastically. "But how are we going to get to Drumheller?"

Robyn grinned. "Easy. Hailey's mom lives there. Do you think your mom would let us hang out at her house? You and I could have a sleepover."

"Well...I don't know..." Hailey hesitated. "I don't think that's such a good idea..."

"What about me and Nick?" I asked.

"You guys could camp in a tent in the backyard," Robyn suggested.

"It's a little cold outside," Nick pointed out.

"So what?" Robyn shrugged. "You have a sleeping bag."

"Thanks for your concern," said Nick. "You and Hailey will be sipping hot chocolate in front of the TV while Trevor and I freeze our butts off."

"It's not *that* cold. Besides, it's in the name of justice," Robyn said. "Please, Hailey? You do want to help your mom, don't you?"

"Of course!" Hailey answered with conviction. A bright flush stained her cheeks.

"Great!" Robyn's eyes brightened. "Could we go tonight?"

"No. It's Thursday. I don't think my mom would let us miss school," said Hailey.

"Tomorrow then," Robyn said.

Hailey bit her bottom lip. "I don't know. I'd have to ask…"

Mr. Joe breezed in at last. "Hey, kids, sorry I'm late. I was on the phone with the museum. There's going to be quite a celebration out there this weekend, because of the new finds." He turned to the white board and began writing.

"Exactly…" Nick paused, his voice low. "There's a press conference being held Saturday morning at the dig site. I saw it on the museum's website."

"Well, if any funny stuff is going on, it'll happen before the conference," I said.

"We'll be there." Robyn took Nick's newspaper and flapped it for emphasis. "And we'll be ready."

The flashlight cast wavering shadows on the grasses beside the path. Gravel crunched under our feet.

"Does someone want to tell me why we couldn't do this in daylight?" Nick said, tripping over a bush.

"Because there are always people around in the daytime. Mr. Joe wouldn't plant the fossils at the dig while someone's watching, doofus," Robyn hissed. "And if he's going to set up another discovery, it has to be before the press conference tomorrow. Can you imagine the headlines if they found another rare fossil right in front of the media? There's no way the dig would be refused funding. No, it's got to be tonight. Mr. Joe was in class with us all week. There's no way he made it out to Drumheller before now."

"How much farther?" I whispered.

"Not far," answered Hailey nervously. She directed the flashlight's beam ahead of us.

"Keep the light down," I advised. "We don't want to give any warning that we're coming."

"There aren't...you know...bears out here, are there?" Nick glanced into the darkness.

"Not likely," Hailey said. "They like the mountains, where there's more food for them. There could be cougars though."

"C-c-cougars?" Nick cleared his throat.

"Sure. There's lots of small game. Gophers and rabbits. Good hunting for coyotes, and maybe the odd cougar." Hailey smiled at Nick's nervousness. "Don't worry though. They don't usually eat people."

"Very comforting," Nick muttered.

It was warm, in spite of the autumn darkness. The moon was just a sliver. We had to rely on the flashlight to guide us over the gnarled path.

"Shhh!" Hailey cautioned. We reached the stairs down the hillside to the dig site. The rickety wood structure creaked underfoot, but we crept down carefully. There was no sign of anyone.

"Let's hide over here." Hailey motioned to a groove in the hill, near an overflowing trash can. It smelled pretty bad, but it was the only hiding spot nearby.

"Whew!" Robyn pinched her nose and breathed through her mouth. "Someone forgot to empty that."

"No kidding." I tried not to gag on the odor of stale French fries and rotting leftovers.

We settled down to wait. The stink made things uncomfortable, but after a while a breeze blew up, and the smell was a little more bearable. We fell silent. Night noises filled the badlands, but in the valley of the dig site, things were very still.

I closed my eyes and yawned. Surveillance sure could be boring. If it weren't for the stench of that garbage, I probably would have fallen asleep.

Hailey checked her watch. "We've been here for half an hour," she said. "How long should we stay?"

"At least another hour," Robyn answered. "It's not that late."

A soft shuffling reached my ears. I sat up and listened hard. The others were alert too, but no one moved.

"Mr. Joe?" Robyn mouthed. I nodded, but Hailey looked absolutely frozen in terror. I strained to hear the sound of footsteps.

The shuffling continued. I peered around the edge of the garbage can but saw nothing in the darkness. Something was definitely making noise though. It was coming nearer every second. I pulled my camera out of my pack. To catch Mr. Joe in the act, we'd have to ambush him. I motioned for the others.

"Trevor, no!" Hailey gave a strangled cry.

Too late. I bounded out from behind the trash can, pressing the photo button on the camera. The flash went off, flooding the clearing in a brief second of blinding light. Mr. Joe was nowhere in sight. I fumbled for the flashlight, clicking it on.

In the same instant, the source of the shuffling noise popped its small furry head out of the crumpled lunch bag it had been probing. It glared at me with tiny black eyes and whirled with its black and white tail raised.

Chapter Eleven

"Skunk!" I yelled. I leaped backward, tripping and crashing into Nick and Robyn, who were crouched directly behind me.

"Ooof!" Robyn wheezed as Nick stumbled and I fell on top of them both. That saved us. We tumbled in a heap behind the trash can just as the skunk sprayed.

A cloud of vile stink wafted into the air. We scrambled up and sprinted for the stairs before the skunk could re-aim. He scuttled into the brush bordering the dig.

"Blech!" Nick coughed as we climbed the stairs at top speed. "What a reek!"

"We're lucky we didn't actually get hit," Hailey said as we reached the top. Only a faint odor followed us. "That skunk was probably trying to get at the garbage, and Trevor scared the heck out of it."

"*I* scared *it*?" I said.

"Yeah. If you hadn't pounced at it, it probably would have just backed away," Hailey answered. She wiped the perspiration from her forehead and pulled off her fleece jacket. We were all sweating from the climb up the hill and the reaction to the skunk.

"You want to put that in my back-pack?" I asked Hailey. I'd brought the backpack along for the camera, which had turned out to be useless. There would be no photos of Mr. Joe planting more fossils that he could take credit for finding. Instead, all I had was a picture—probably blurry—of an extremely ticked-off skunk. I wondered if *National Geographic* would pay me for that one. It wasn't much to show for a nighttime trek in the middle of nowhere.

"Sure." Hailey stuffed her fleece into the zippered pocket and then took the flashlight, shining it on the path ahead.

A few minutes' hard walking brought us to the path near the road out of the park. Hailey's house was only another twenty minutes away.

When we reached her gate, she led us around to the backyard, where our flimsy tent swayed in the wind.

"Well, guys. I guess that's it," Hailey said, almost cheerfully. "We didn't bust Mr. Joe. Maybe the discoveries at the dig are legitimate, after all. Mr. Joe could have taken the fossils to sell privately, you know. He'd probably get a lot of money for them."

I wondered why Hailey didn't seem disappointed, but then it was obvious. If the finds were real, then there was a good chance the funding would come through and her mom would continue to work out here. But it just didn't seem probable to me. The Ichthylobuttosaur had never been found in this valley—nowhere else had that dinosaur been discovered except in South Dakota. The coincidence was too much. I just knew it.

"See you in the morning," Robyn said.

Nick eyed the shabby tent with distaste. "If we survive the night in that thing."

Bright sunshine shone through the tent's fabric, waking me from an uncomfortable sleep. The morning cold seeped inside, and the sides of the tent were damp with condensation. Nick had his sleeping bag pulled up around his ears. Only the spikes of his black hair showed through the opening. I nudged him.

"Nick! Get up!" I glanced at my watch. "The press conference starts in less than an hour."

Nick poked his head out of the sleeping bag, blinked and yawned. "Remind me to choose something else when I start thinking about a career. Detectives never get any sleep."

I crawled out of the sleeping bag, shivering, and pulled on my clothes. Outside, it was a beautiful fall morning.

Hailey poked her head out the back door. "Hey, sleepyheads," she sang out. "We've been up for ages. Come and have some hot chocolate."

At the words *hot chocolate*, Nick bolted out of bed, threw on his clothes and ran barefoot to the house, leaving me holding the tent flap open.

"Leave some for me!" I grabbed my backpack and shoes and followed Nick inside.

After breakfast and the promised hot chocolate, we got cleaned up and waited impatiently for Hailey's parents. Her mom was driving everyone to the dig. She would be one of the spokespeople meeting with reporters, so she dressed a little more carefully, with her hair pulled back neatly.

We piled into the van, and the short drive took only a few minutes. The parking lot was crowded. Among the cars were a number of news vehicles emblazoned with the logos of their employers. All the major news outlets in the province seemed to be here. There were trucks, vans and suvs from

Calgary, Edmonton, Medicine Hat, Lethbridge and Drumheller. A bunch of rental vehicles piled with equipment showed that some reporters came from farther away.

Hailey turned to her mom in alarm. "Where did all these people come from?"

"Some from as far away as the States. This is a big deal," Hailey's mom answered. She smoothed her hair and got out of the car. "Let's go."

We made yet another trip down the plywood stairs. A large crowd had gathered at the bottom and was fighting for the best vantage point to take pictures and live video. Mr. Joe was already there, looking nervous but pleased.

"Hi Jamie," he said to Hailey's mom. "This has been a huge success. There's even a news crew here from South Dakota. They were very interested in the Ichthylobuttosaur fossils."

"Good," Hailey's mom answered. "You kids go stand off to the side, where you'll be out of the way." She wrinkled her nose. "What is that gosh-awful stink? We must have had a skunk visit last night."

Nick, Robyn and I exchanged guilty glances. Hailey was too busy eyeing the reporters to pay attention. She kept rubbing her hands over the goose bumps on her bare arms.

"Hailey, you want your jacket?" I asked. "It's still in my backpack." We moved to the side, to give Mr. Joe and Hailey's mom a small section where they could discuss the discovery. The reporters began asking questions, and Hailey's mom had to raise her voice to be heard among the whirring and clicking of cameras.

"Sure." Hailey didn't even glance at me. A thickset man with short legs bounced forward, waving his hand at Hailey's mom.

"Ma'am!" he called out. "I'm from the *Argus Leader*, in South Dakota. Can you tell me how it is that Ichthylobuttosaur has never yet been discovered here in Alberta? What is it about this site that is so significant for this particular dinosaur?"

Hailey's mom launched into a complicated speech about the habitat of the Ichthylobuttosaur, while I pulled Hailey's jacket out of the bag and handed it to her. A small piece of paper that had been stuck to the jacket fell to the ground. I picked it up and took a closer look. It was blue and white and scrunched together, with adhesive coating on one side. Fuzz from Hailey's jacket clung to the exposed sticky surfaces.

It looked familiar. As I untwisted it, I recognized it.

Hailey's eyes widened when she saw what was in my hands.

It was the label from the bag of fossils from the University of South Dakota.

Chapter Twelve

"Where did you get this?" I hissed under the babble of voices as reporters volleyed questions at Hailey's mother. I waved the crumpled label at Hailey. The words *Ichthy. butt.* were still clearly typed on the front. There was no question it was the label from Mr. Joe's missing bag of fossils.

Hailey turned pale and tried to snatch the label from me. I jerked my hand away. Suddenly a whole bunch of facts hurtled through my brain. I couldn't believe I'd been so stupid. Why hadn't we suspected Hailey before?

She had just as much reason as Mr. Joe to want the dig to succeed. She'd told us that her mom might have to get a job somewhere else, that they might have to move.

Hailey had walked into the classroom just as Robyn was trying to find the fund-raiser forms after the school carnival. Hailey would have seen the fossils inside the filing cabinet. She would have known which ones were the most valuable. She could have stashed the others somewhere so she could shift the blame for the theft to Robyn.

"It's not what you think," Hailey stammered. Robyn and Nick listened intently. "I know it looks bad, but I didn't have anything to do with those fossils. The label must have caught on my sleeve…"

I found myself wanting to believe her. After all, I didn't have any real evidence. And then, in one blinding moment, I realized that I did. One small fact that had bothered me weeks ago suddenly made sense.

"You are lying!" I said through gritted teeth. "And I can prove it."

Hailey's eyes widened. "What do you mean?"

"Tell me about Robyn's prediction again," I answered.

"She told me to beware of yellow school buses," Hailey said uneasily.

"And what happened?"

"The bus pulled up in front of the school, and I tripped and dropped my backpack. The bus ran right over it. Ruined everything." Hailey crossed her arms in front of her chest defensively.

"Everything?"

"Everything!" Hailey flared.

"Including the science booklet that was due that morning?"

Hailey hesitated.

"We were supposed to work on that booklet together, Hailey. And you left it until the last minute. I helped you finish it on the field-trip bus ride—after everything in your backpack was supposedly destroyed. But your homework and your binder were in perfect condition. How did that happen?"

"I...uh, forgot them at school..." Hailey was obviously thinking rapidly.

"Wrong. You told me on the bus you'd brought it home with you. So you were either lying then, or you're lying now. I'm going to guess you pulled that homework out because it was worth half our marks, before you deliberately threw your backpack into the path of the bus."

"Why would I do that? That's ridiculous!" Hailey's voice squeaked. "What does any of this have to do with the fossils?"

"You were trying to set up Robyn," I said. "One more fantastic prediction was enough to have kids really believing that Robyn had psychic powers. Then you wrote an anonymous note that threatened to expose her as a fake, so Robyn would 'find' the fossils. That way you could make it look like Robyn ripped them off."

"You did that?" Incensed, Robyn turned to Hailey. "I thought you were my friend!" she spat.

Hailey's face was white to the lips. Around us, the press conference flowed on. The reporters hadn't twigged to the extraordinary conversation unfolding in their midst. The reporter from South Dakota was peppering Hailey's mother with a line of questions.

"Are you sure, Dr. Ross, that the findings in this remarkable discovery are absolutely certain to be authentic?" he was saying.

I fixed Hailey with a menacing glare. "*You're* the one who came out here and planted those fossils. Not Mr. Joe. You knew it would rock the science world. You didn't care about the dig at all— you just wanted to save your mother's job!" I accused.

"That's not true!" Hailey shrieked, tears coursing down her cheeks. "I did care about the dig! I never thought about it being a fake discovery until it was too late. I never knew what *Itchy butt* meant, and I had no idea that everyone would think this was the greatest discovery in the whole world!"

Hailey's cries had interrupted the press conference. Every reporter turned to look at us. Camera crews pointed the lenses away from Hailey's mother and onto us instead. Everyone in that creepy, expectant silence waited, pens poised, cameras rolling. Hailey looked like a trapped animal.

Hailey's mother stood with her mouth half open. "Hailey! You can't be serious," she exclaimed in horror.

"Are you saying," the reporter from South Dakota said slowly, his eyes narrowing, "that this whole thing is a hoax? That we've been led out here to break the paleontology story of the decade, only to find out it's a lie?"

Hailey covered her face with her hands. "I'm sorry! I just buried the fossils at the site because I thought that if more fossils turned up, the funding would come through. I'm tired of my mom moving to where the best jobs are. I didn't want to move *again*!" She choked down a sob.

"Hailey…" Hailey's mother struggled to speak. She paused for a painful moment, then sighed. "I don't even know what to say."

"How did a kid like you get your hands on such valuable fossils?" one reporter asked Hailey.

"I can answer that," Mr. Joe broke in. "I had borrowed some fossils from the University of South Dakota. They were with some others from Drumheller I was using in Hailey's class."

"So you did steal them!" Nick exclaimed.

"No, I didn't!" Mr. Joe rounded on him. "They were on loan to me."

"Then why did we see an article in the paper about fossils being stolen from the same university?" I asked. "Seems like more than a coincidence, when you had a bag of them hidden in your filing cabinet!"

"It was a misunderstanding," Mr. Joe said, his face reddening. "I've already straightened it out with the university.

Remember I said I was developing a new method for dating fossils? Well, I needed fossils to experiment with, and so I borrowed a bag from the storeroom. My professor had told me to take a few that weren't needed, and these ones hadn't been touched in years. I didn't realize they were important—the *Ichthy. butt.* abbreviation on the label didn't register with me. Should have, I guess. But the Ichthylobuttosaur isn't a well-known dinosaur."

While the group digested this information, Mrs. Ross regained her composure. Furious, she fixed a hard stare at Hailey. "I'm extremely sorry that the actions of my daughter have caused you all to waste a trip out here for nothing," she said. "I'm sure Hailey didn't intend for things to go this far. I'm sorry you don't have a story to take back to your editors."

"Are you kidding?" the South Dakota reporter said with relish. "Fraud, a fake dig site and a kid behind the whole thing? This story is even better! This might even go national."

Hailey froze, her face panicked. "No!"

"Will the museum press charges?" another reporter asked.

"I can't speak for the museum in this instance," said Hailey's mother firmly. "We have no further comment at this time." She stepped away from the crowd, took Hailey's shoulder and propelled her up the rickety steps to the parking area. As they disappeared, the press crews turned to Mr. Joe and us.

"Do you have anything to say about this?" a reporter asked Mr. Joe.

"Are you kids friends of Hailey's? Were you in on this with her?" Someone shoved a tape recorder under Robyn's nose.

"How did you know that she planted the fossils?" a television reporter asked me. The light from the camera glared into my face.

"I...uh..." My mind went blank. "Well, if it hadn't been for that skunk..."

Mr. Joe stepped forward. "Please." He held up his hand. "We can't say anything more right now." He herded Nick, Robyn and me toward the steps before anyone could say more. I looked back as we started up the stairs.

The television anchorperson scratched his head. "What skunk?" He shouted after me. "Hey, kid! What skunk?"

"The one that helped me solve the mystery, of course!" I called back, and I grinned at his confusion.

Chapter Thirteen

"Some friends you guys turned out to be," Robyn said at the bus stop Monday morning. "I can't believe you and Nick actually thought I took the fossils."

"You have to admit, it looked bad," I told her. "We caught you red-handed. What else were we supposed to think?"

"You could have trusted me." Robyn gave me a grumpy look.

"Well, the evidence was against you," I replied. "But I didn't think you took them for yourself...I figured you had some plan to help the dig."

"Well, still." Robyn looked miffed.

Nick jogged around the corner, another newspaper tucked under his arm. "Did you guys see this?" he asked, stopping in front of us. "My dad was reading it this morning and left it for me." He shook the paper open to exhibit the front page.

Prominent Paleontologist's Daughter Admits to Fossil Fraud

The science world is reeling after an important paleontological dig site in Drumheller has been revealed as a fake. While several authentic fossils have been discovered in the soil, a prominent paleontologist's daughter has admitted to planting Ichthylobuttosaur fossils at the site in a misguided attempt to get more funding. The Ichthylobuttosaur has never before been discovered in Alberta. The name of the underage girl cannot be released. No charges have been laid at this time.

The newspaper article went on to describe in detail the nature of the dig and Hailey's confession at the press conference.

"Yikes." Robyn winced. "Now everyone in the whole world knows. Hailey must feel horrible."

"I still want to know what the skunk had to do with it," Nick said.

Robyn turned to me as well. "Me too," she said.

"That's easy," I answered. "Hailey shouted 'No!' when I jumped out from behind the trash can. Remember how she stayed hidden? Why would she do that, if she thought we were about to catch Mr. Joe? I bet she guessed those noises were made by an animal, because there wasn't a culprit to catch. She knew that the whole stakeout was a sham."

"So she tried to warn you before you got eaten," Nick said. "Thoughtful of her."

Robyn sighed. "I'm still mad at Hailey, but I'm glad they aren't pressing charges or printing her name. I thought *I'd* be humiliated if Hailey spread rumors at school that I wasn't really psychic, but this is a hundred times worse."

"I don't see why you cared anyway," Nick said. "You kept saying you couldn't really tell fortunes, so I don't see what the big deal was."

"Because everyone started to believe that I could," Robyn explained. "It made no difference what I said. And everyone would have been mad at me if they believed I was a fake. Rumors can hurt. A lot." She paused for emphasis.

"People don't think of them as a weapon, but they are."

"Okay, well. After that heavy piece of wisdom, I guess you've given up fortune-telling for good," Nick commented.

"Not quite," Robyn said slowly. "I think I have one more left."

"You do?" I said, surprised.

"What is it?" Nick wanted to know.

Robyn gave us a mysterious smile. "I predict...that Trevor's going to fail science."

I reacted with shock. "Why?" I asked. "How could you possibly know that?"

"Remember that homework assignment you worked on with Hailey? The one that helped you figure out she was setting me up? The one worth half your grade?" Robyn said.

"Yeah," I answered.

Robyn reached into her backpack, pulled out several rumpled sheets of paper and gave them to me. I blinked as I recognized my own handwriting. "You never handed it in," she said. "You forgot it on the bus!"

Michele Martin Bossley has written numerous books for kids, including *Swiped, Cracked* and *Bio-pirate*, all mysteries in the Orca Currents series that feature Robyn, Nick and Trevor. Michele lives in Calgary, Alberta.

orca *currents*

For more information on all the books
in the Orca Currents series, please visit
www.orcabook.com